Hannah's Tall Order

AN A TO Z SANDWICH

WRITTEN BY **LINDA VANDER HEYDEN**

ILLUSTRATED BY **KAYLA HARREN**

When Hannah was hungry and wanted to munch,
She'd stop at McDougal's to order some lunch.

Now Hannah was tiny (in fact, quite petite),
But don't let that fool you. Oh boy—could she eat!

Whistling a tune, Hannah swung the door wide.
"Oh no," groaned McDougal. "She's coming inside!"

"Hi, Mr. McDougal! Guess what?" Hannah said.

"I've come for a sandwich on thick whole wheat bread...."

"An A to Z sandwich!" young Hannah declared.
An alphabet sandwich? McDougal just stared.

"I'd like…"

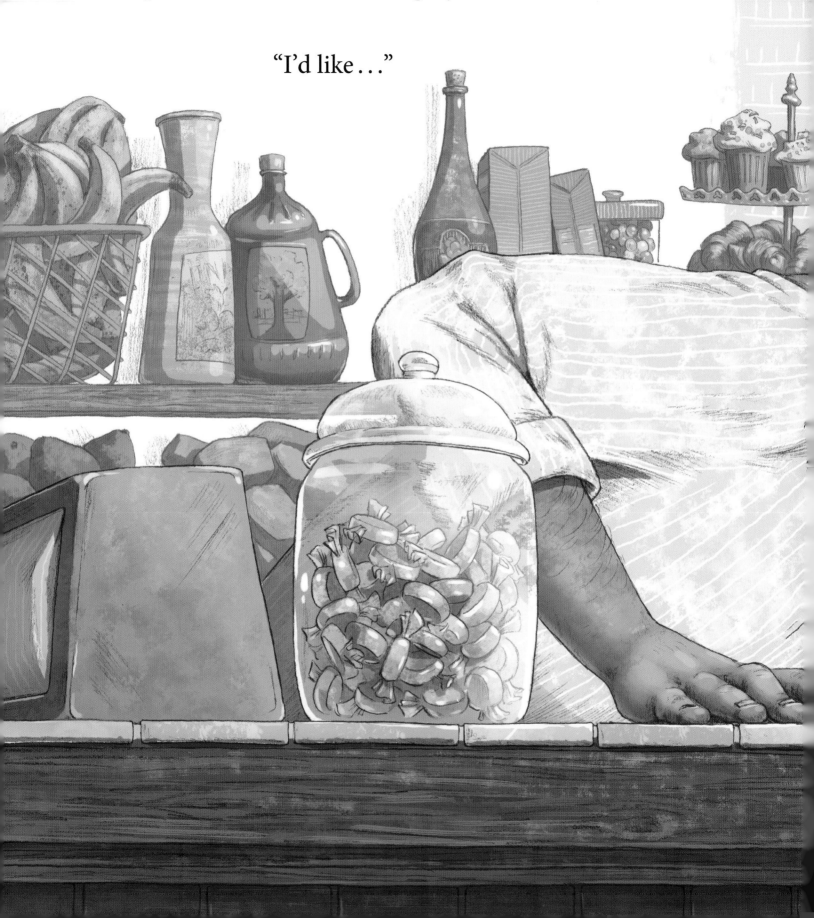

"Avocados and bean sprouts—fresh carrots galore. Dill pickles, egg salad—those figs I adore!"

McDougal got busy and started to chop.

He peeled and he minced. He grated nonstop!

"Green peppers," said Hannah. "Sliced thin, if you please.
And drizzle on lots of sweet honey from bees.

"Add ice cream and jelly—then ketchup (two plops),
A freshly squeezed lemon—just ten tiny drops."

"A dollop or two of **marshmallow** Fluff…

It's right there on your shelf—the white, sticky stuff!"

"And if you don't mind, I'd like lots of **nuts**, too.
I'm not all that hungry—one **olive** will do."

McDougal turned red. He broke out in a sweat.
Hannah pointed her finger. She wasn't done yet!

"A slice of **potato**. Or better yet . . . two!
And sprinkle on **quinoa**. It's grown in Peru."

"A **radish** to give it the zip that it needs. . . .
Then toss on a handful of **sunflower seeds**."

"A ripe red **tomato** picked fresh off the vine.
And **ugli** fruit chopped up especially fine."

"**Vanilla** and **whipped** cream—for flavor and flare!"

"Oh no!" Hannah giggled. "You whip-creamed your hair!"

McDougal looked cross and he started to shake.

"How much more," he asked Hannah,

"can this sandwich take?"

Hannah hopped on a stool and she gave it a spin.
"I know what it's missing!" she said with a grin.

"Please add a small helping of fresh **xouba** fish.
I've heard that it's healthy—and oh, so deeelish!

"Then spread on a layer of creamy mooshed **yam**…
and grated **zucchini**—no more than a gram."

McDougal said, "Finally—it's ready to eat!
I had to use white bread. I'm out of whole wheat."

"What?" Hannah said. "Only white bread? Oh ack!
In that case, you'll just have to put it all BACK!"

For my friend Jeannie–who can build a
grilled cheese sandwich in no time flat

–Love, L. V.

Mom and Dad, thank you for
your love and support.
–K. H.